DOUG THE STEAM SHOVEL

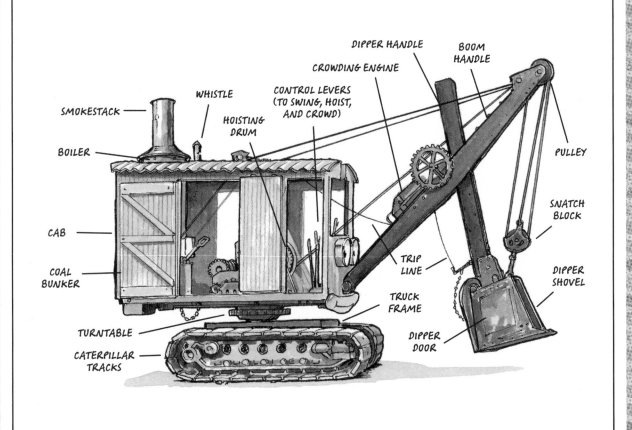

SMOKESTACK

WHISTLE

DIPPER HANDLE

CROWDING ENGINE

BOOM HANDLE

BOILER

HOISTING DRUM

CONTROL LEVERS
(TO SWING, HOIST,
AND CROWD)

PULLEY

CAB

SNATCH
BLOCK

COAL
BUNKER

TRIP
LINE

DIPPER
SHOVEL

TRUCK
FRAME

TURNTABLE

DIPPER
DOOR

CATERPILLAR
TRACKS

TRACTOR MAC

CERTIFICATE OF REGISTRATION

• • •

_____

ALSO BY BILLY STEERS

TRACTOR MAC
TEAMWORK

Written and illustrated by
BILLY STEERS

FARRAR STRAUS GIROUX • NEW YORK

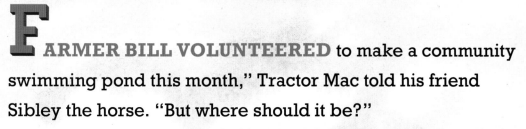

"F ARMER BILL VOLUNTEERED to make a community swimming pond this month," Tractor Mac told his friend Sibley the horse. "But where should it be?"

"The old mill pond site has filled in over time, but it would make a nice place for swimming and picnics," said Sibley.

"I have a plan," said Farmer Bill. "But since the stream will keep flowing, we'll have to reroute the water before we can dig. This will be a lot of work."

"We'll all pitch in," said Tractor Mac to his friends.

Jobs were handed out for the project, and the team began the task.

Haul.

Dig.

Push. Grade.

Rake. **Smooth.**

Sibley, Doug the steam shovel, Carl the bulldozer, Daisy, and Tractor Mac made a very good team. Within a few days, much of the new pond was dug.

"Important jobs kept me away, but you can all relax now!" boomed a loud voice. "Deke the tractor is here just in time!"

"You know how to build swimming holes, Deke?" asked Tractor Mac.

"I'm the best at building everything!
Little lakes are easy!" crowed Deke.

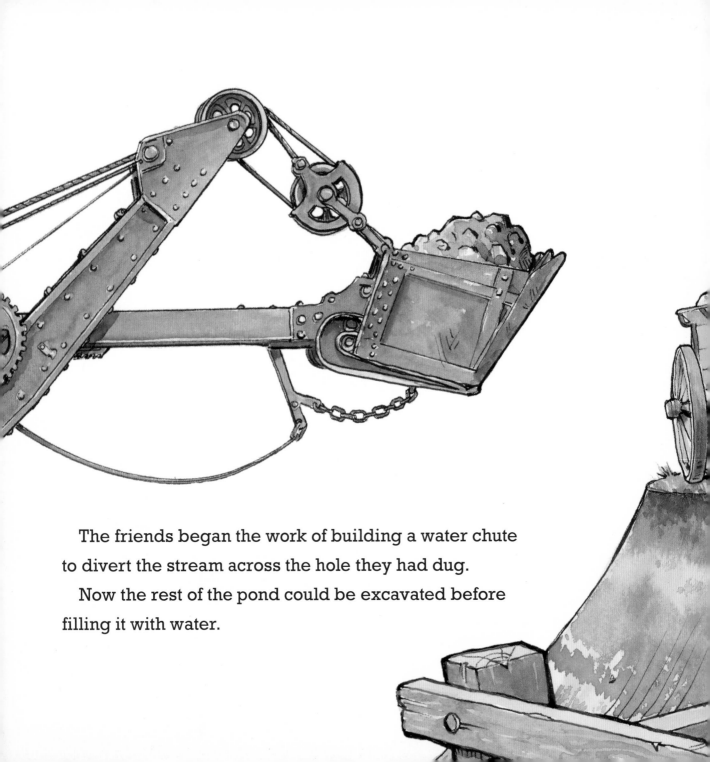

The friends began the work of building a water chute
to divert the stream across the hole they had dug.

Now the rest of the pond could be excavated before
filling it with water.

"I'll haul that for you, Sibley," said Deke.

"You're not hauling correctly."

The group kept on digging.

"I'll push those rocks for you, little yellow dozer," Deke said to Carl. "You're moving rocks all wrong."

"Tiny red tractor, you're not raking the ground properly," Deke said to Daisy. "I'll do it the right way for you."

The hole for the new pond got bigger.

"Take a break, old-timer, before you hurt yourself," Deke said to Doug. "I'll show you the Deke way to use a shovel!"

"Why are you all out of the pit?" Tractor Mac asked his friends.

"Deke told us he was better at digging projects, and he took over our jobs," said Daisy sadly.

"Deke, can we talk about working with others?"
asked Tractor Mac.

"Not now. I don't like how you've done the grading here,
and it's up to me to make it right," grunted Deke.

"Be careful of the supports, Deke!" shouted Tractor Mac.
But it was too late.

Deke's tire hit the water chute. Down came the structure. In rushed the water.

"I'm stuck in the mud! Help!" cried Deke.

Tractor Mac and his friends acted quickly. The water was rising fast!

Sibley and Tractor Mac pulled and hauled to free
Deke. Carl piled up rocks to slow the flow of water.

Doug used his bucket and cables to hoist Deke out of
the deepening lake. Daisy used her rake to get Deke's
driver to safety.

"Thank you all," said Deke a little shakily.
"I'm sorry I tried to do everything myself.
I should have let you all handle your own jobs."

"That's what teamwork is, Deke. Everyone doing their own small part to finish a big job," said Tractor Mac. "Now we need someone to create a beach area. Can you do that?"

"I'd like to do my small part," said Deke.
And he did. Together they finished the new pond,
working as a team.

To the Screaming Eagle and Rhody Red
Airlift Squadrons—Teamwork 24/7

Farrar Straus Giroux Books for Young Readers
175 Fifth Avenue, New York 10010

Copyright © 2016 by Billy Steers
All rights reserved
Color separations by Bright Arts (H.K.) Ltd.
Printed in China by Toppan Leefung Printing Ltd.,
Dongguan City, Guangdong Province
Designed by Kristie Radwilowicz
First Farrar Straus Giroux edition, 2016
1   3   5   7   9   10   8   6   4   2

mackids.com

Library of Congress Cataloging-in-Publication Data
[TK]

Our books may be purchased in bulk for promotional, educational, or business use.
Please contact your local bookseller or the Macmillan Corporate and Premium Sales Department
at (800) 221-7945 x5442 or by e-mail at MacmillanSpecialMarkets@macmillan.com.

ABOUT THE AUTHOR

Billy Steers is an author, illustrator, and commercial pilot. In addition to the Tractor Mac series, he has worked on forty other children's books. Mr. Steers had horses and sheep on the farm where he grew up in Connecticut. Married with three sons, he still lives in Connecticut. Learn more about the Tractor Mac books at www.tractormac.com.

TRACTOR MAC

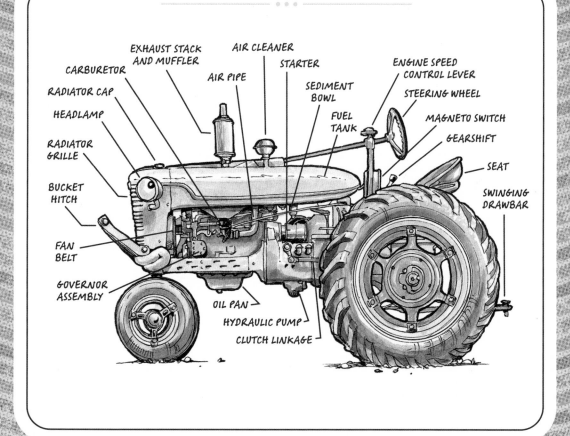

CARBURETOR

EXHAUST STACK
AND MUFFLER

AIR CLEANER

AIR PIPE

STARTER

ENGINE SPEED
CONTROL LEVER

RADIATOR CAP

SEDIMENT
BOWL

STEERING WHEEL

HEADLAMP

FUEL
TANK

MAGNETO SWITCH

GEARSHIFT

RADIATOR
GRILLE

SEAT

BUCKET
HITCH

SWINGING
DRAWBAR

FAN
BELT

GOVERNOR
ASSEMBLY

OIL PAN

HYDRAULIC PUMP

CLUTCH LINKAGE